Goose the Bear

Katja Gehrmann

Translated by
Connie Stradling Morby

SKY PONY PRESS
NEW YORK

In a forest in Canada, a fox lurked behind a tree. He wanted to give his wife a special present, so he had been watching a colony of geese for a while. When the time was right, he stole an almost-hatched egg.

"What a delicious surprise it will be when a roast goose hatches for dinner."

He started running with the egg under his arm, satisfied with himself.

He was so excited that he forgot to be careful where he was going . . .

. . . and ran into a bear!

"Watch it, you red walking stick!" growled the bear,
annoyed.

Frightened, the fox ran away. Bears were not to be
messed with.

As the bear picked himself up, he eyed something
big and white.

Curious, he picked it up, wondering what it was.

I'll take it with me, he thought. *Fox must have lost
it. Where did he find such an interesting thing?*

The bear didn't hear the soft
knocking from inside the egg.

"Mama!" peeped a small animal, whose head was sticking out of the egg.

Startled, the bear looked at the little animal.

He looked all around. No one was in sight.

Oh my, he thought. *What should I do with this thing?*

"You wait here until your mother comes," he said. Then the bear left without looking back. He felt bad but didn't want to be a babysitter. And fox would probably make fun of him if he stayed.

"Mama!" called the animal, as she jumped into the bear's arms.

"Mama!"

"Just a minute," growled the bear. "I am not your mama! I'm a bear. And you're a . . . well, you are definitely not a bear."

"Yes, Mama," said the little animal.

"I'm not your mama," said the bear again. "I'm big and strong, have a brown coat, and like to catch salmon. And you're—different."

"Yes, Mama," said the little animal.

She doesn't understand at all! the bear thought. *I'll have to show her what a real bear can do instead.*

"Now pay attention. There are things you can't do because you're not a bear. I'm going to show you how well bears climb trees."

The bear started to climb.
"Mama!" called the little creature sadly. She tried to climb up behind, but kept slipping off the tree trunk.
"See!" the bear called down from the top.

CAUTIO

BEARS

"Mama!" the animal cried desperately and flapped her wings. Amazingly, she started to fly. She flapped harder . . .

. . . and reached the top of the tree.

"Mama!" she gasped.

"That just can't be . . ." the bear stammered. "So, you can climb. But that still doesn't make you a bear."

"We bears are fast runners," said the bear. "Just watch!"
He started running.
Now the little creature will have to know that she isn't a bear, he thought.

After he had run a good distance, he sat down in the grass,
panting. *That'll do it*, he thought.

"Mama," called the little animal . . .

. . . and dashed behind the bear.

The bear couldn't believe his eyes. This creature was so fast that it hardly touched the ground.

"Unbelievable!" he growled.

"Mama!" the animal said.

The bear was perplexed. This little creature could climb and run like a bear, but she looked entirely different. *Some animals change when they get big, though*, the bear thought. Did he look like that when he was little? Did bears hatch out of eggs? He had always thought bears were special, but now, he wasn't sure how.

All he knew was that he was a bear—a strong, dangerous bear to be feared. And this little animal was starting to get on his nerves. She was really sweet, but he couldn't waste his whole day with her.

The bear needed a cool bath.
He felt confused.

So he jumped into the river. Now the animal would finally realize that he wasn't her mother. He looked up, and to his horror, the creature called, "Mama," and jumped.

Oh no! What if she sinks? thought the bear, terrified, and he swam back.

"Oh no, I'm too late! It was such a nice little . . . oh my,"
growled the bear sadly. He could only see a few bubbles where
the animal had dived into the water.

Then a head popped up.

"Mama!" spluttered the creature.

Unbelievable! thought the bear, relieved. *It climbs like a bear and runs like a bear and swims like a bear.*

"Hmm . . . you still have to grow a lot and get stronger before you look like me," he growled.

They swam side by side for a while.

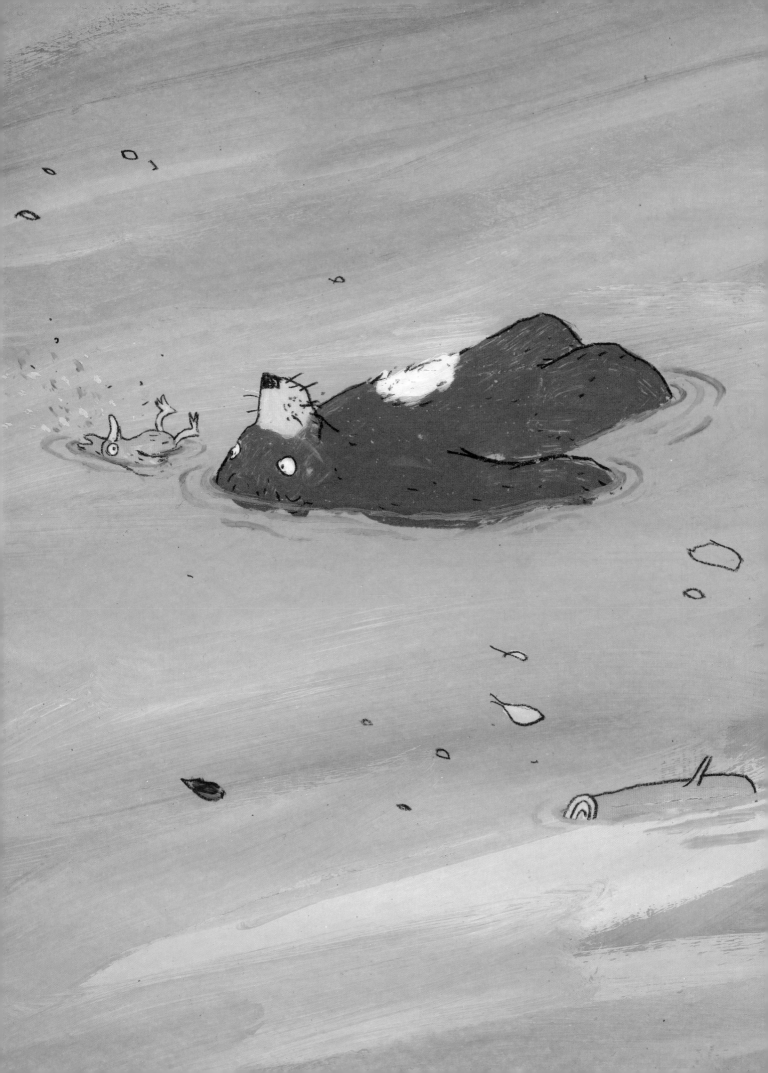

The bear was very tired.
But the little animal wanted to catch salmon.
"Mama?" she asked.
"Zzzzz," snored the bear.
The animal jumped onto a stone and watched the
salmon swimming by.

She quickly caught a magnificent salmon and bit down hard on
its tail. But how was she supposed to get it onto land?
Along came the fox.

The salmon jumped wildly . . .

. . . and hit the fox in the head.

When the bear came running to the river bank, he was surprised.

"That's fabulous! You caught such a big fish! And you showed that fox!"

This little animal was strong. The bear was proud.
It *could* be his child.

The fox rubbed his throbbing head.

"Well, you red ragbag, you'd better think ahead of time if you want to pick a fight with us bears. Even if they're little, and even if they have beaks," the bear yelled to the fox.

The fox rubbed his head again.

I'm glad I didn't take that goose home after all. She's too much like a bear, he thought as he made his way home.

First English-language edition by Sky Pony Press, 2014.
English translation copyright © 2014 by Skyhorse Publishing, Inc.

Sky Pony Press books may be purchased in bulk at special discounts for sales
promotion, corporate gifts, fund-raising, or educational purposes. Special editions
can also be created to specifications. For details, contact the Special Sales
Department, Sky Pony Press, 307 West 36th Street, 11th Floor, New York, NY 10018 or
info@skyhorsepublishing.com.

Sky Pony® is a registered trademark of Skyhorse Publishing, Inc.®, a Delaware
corporation.

Visit our website at www.skyponypress.com.

10 9 8 7 6 5 4 3 2 1

Manufactured in China, September 2013
This product conforms to CPSIA 2008

Library of Congress Cataloging-in-Publication Data is available on file.

ISBN: 978-1-62636-384-7